Tales of the Caribbean

Anansi Stories

Told by Evan Jones

Contents

Illustrated by

Bob Bowdige page 3

Mary Davey pages 23, 24/25, 26, 27, 28/29 and 30

Stephen Holmes pages 4 and 5

Gail Lewton pages 14/15, 17, 18, 19, 20, 21 and 22

Doreen McGuiness pages 6/7, 8/9, 10/11 and 13

Jenny Northway pages 31, 32, 33, 34/35, 36/37, 38, 39, 40,
41, 42, 43, 45, 46/47 and 48

Who is Anansi?

Anansi is a spider. Anansi is a man. Anansi is a spider man. Stories of Anansi were told by the people of West Africa and brought by West African slaves to the West Indies.

Now the thing about Anansi is this: he may be weak, he may be ugly, he may be lazy, mean, selfish, lying, wicked, cunning, or any one of a million names you want to call him, but Anansi is smart. He is smarter than all the others, and he lives by his wits. And one more thing about Anansi: he loves a joke.

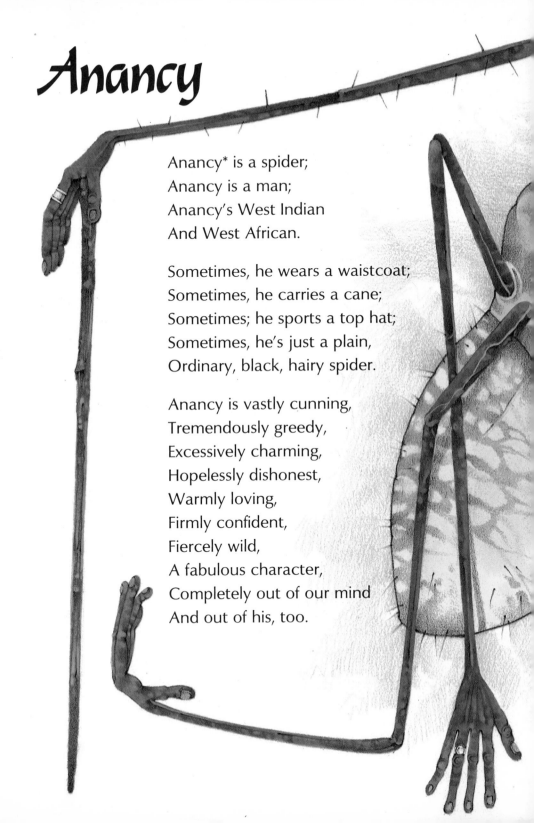

Anancy

Anancy* is a spider;
Anancy is a man;
Anancy's West Indian
And West African.

Sometimes, he wears a waistcoat;
Sometimes, he carries a cane;
Sometimes; he sports a top hat;
Sometimes, he's just a plain,
Ordinary, black, hairy spider.

Anancy is vastly cunning,
Tremendously greedy,
Excessively charming,
Hopelessly dishonest,
Warmly loving,
Firmly confident,
Fiercely wild,
A fabulous character,
Completely out of our mind
And out of his, too.

Anancy is a master planner,
A great user
Of other people's plans;
He pockets everybody's food,
Shelter, land, money, and more;
He achieves mountains of things,
Like stolen flour dumplings;
He deceives millions of people,
Even the man in the moon;
And he solves all the mysteries
On earth, in air, under sea.

And always,
Anancy changes
From a spider into a man
And from a man into a spider
And back again
At the drop of a sleepy eyelid.

Andrew Salkey

* There are several spellings of Anansi's name.

Anansi and Snake

Anansi was a spider, a hairy, black, long-legged spider who lived in the forest. The other animals despised him. He wasn't strong like the Elephant, or brave like the Lion. He wasn't beautiful like the Gazelle or fierce like the Tiger. He couldn't run like the Deer, sing like the Bird, buzz like the Bee, or swim like the Fish. But Anansi was smart.

Anansi was determined that all the other animals should recognize his greatness, so he tried to get into their good books. He would bring presents to the Tiger, and play with his children, praise the Peacock for his feathers or the Ox for his horns; but it didn't work. They still despised him. He was still just Brer Anansi, small, black and hairy.

Anansi had to do something to make the animals respect him. He knew that whatever they said, all of them were afraid of Snake. The Dog and the Rabbit fled from him in terror, and even the Elephant turned aside if he saw Snake hanging from a branch in his way.

One day, all the animals were gathered together, as was the custom, boasting to one another, telling each other of their beauty and strength. When it was Anansi's turn he climbed on a tree trunk and shouted, "I am the most beautiful, I am the strongest of all." The Hyena laughed and the Jackass brayed, and the Monkeys jumped up and down screeching and howling in amusement.

"What can you do, Anansi," said the Tiger, "to prove that you are the strongest?"

All the animals laughed.

"I will capture Snake," boasted Anansi.

All the animals laughed again.

"Anansi," said Tiger, "if you capture Snake, we will agree that you are the strongest. What is more, we will make you the Storyteller. All the animal stories will be called Anansi stories.

"All right," said Anansi, "I'll do it."

Easier said than done. Anansi had bitten off more than he could chew. Boasting was one thing, but capturing Snake was another. Still, he had accepted the challenge, so he had better think of something smart.

Anansi went deep into the forest, where the trees grew tall, and long vines hung from their branches. He cut a length of vine and tied one end of it into a noose. Then he spread out the noose on the path in front of Snake's house, and put some berries in the middle of it. Then holding on to the other end of the vine, he hid behind a tree, and waited. Soon Snake came, slithering and sliding down the path. He stopped when he saw the berries, and put his head right into the noose to eat them. Anansi yanked his end of the vine, and Snake reared up as the noose closed on him, and Anansi was pulled out from behind the tree and right across the path into a prickly bush. Anansi let go, and Snake slithered away.

That was one day. Next morning early Anansi was back in front of Snake's house again. This time he had a spade, and he was digging a hole in Snake's pathway. When the hole was dug, Anansi smeared all the sides of it with grease. Then he covered it up with dry palm leaves, and scattered dirt on them so it looked perfectly natural. Then he sat down behind the tree and waited. Soon Snake came, slithering and sliding down the path. He saw the dusty palm leaves in his way and tapped them lightly with his head. Down they fell into the greasy pit. Snake carried on. He was so long that he just made a bridge of himself, with his head on one side of the pit and his tail on the other, and he slithered away.

That was another day. Next morning early, Anansi was busy again, this time with a saw, a hammer, and some nails. Anansi made a trap, a square box with slatted sides. There was a door in the trap, and the spaces between the slats were just wide enough to allow Snake to crawl in. When the trap was finished Anansi baited it with a bunch of bananas. Soon, Pig came by on his way to the river. He saw the open door, and the bunch of bananas and he went straight in and started happily munching away. Anansi shut the door behind him. Pig paid no attention, enjoying the bananas. He paid no attention while Anansi dragged the trap to the path in front of Snake's house, and left him there.

Anansi had worked out that Snake could get into the cage and eat Pig, but when he'd eaten him his belly would be so big that he couldn't get out. So Anansi sat behind the tree, and waited.

Soon there was the most terrible screeching and howling, and screaming, and crashing and banging, and Pig went by in a cloud of dust. Of course when Pig saw Snake trying to crawl into the cage he was so terrified that he had smashed the cage to smithereens, broke free, and run screaming through the forest. That was another day.

Next morning, Anansi went to the river and cut a long bamboo pole, longer than Snake. He dragged the pole up the pathway to Snake's house. Snake looked out to see what Anansi was doing.

"Morning, Brer Anansi," said Snake.

"Good morning, Snake."

"Anansi," said Snake, "I am beginning to get vexed. One day you make a noose for me, another day you dig a greasy pit, and the next day you come and tease me with a juicy piglet. Why don't you leave me alone?"

"Well," said Brer Anansi, and sugar wouldn't melt in his mouth, "I so much admire you, Mr Snake, so much respect you, I really did mean to give you the Pig as a present."

"Is that so?" said Snake. Then what is the meaning of the greasy pit, and the noose? That is not presents."

"I made a bet," confessed Anansi.

"A bet. What kind of a bet?"

"I had a bet with Tiger that you were the longest Animal in the forest."

"Of course," said Snake.

"Some don't believe it. Some say Crocodile is longer. Some say Giraffe's neck alone is longer than your whole body."

Snake was really vexed now. "Listen to me, Anansi," he said, "why you didn't tell me this from the beginning? Why you messing around with noose and greasy pit?"

"I had to capture you," said Anansi, "to measure you."

"That's all you want to do? Measure me?"

"That is so."

Snake stared at Anansi out of his cold black eyes. "If you lying to me, Anansi, you dead."

Anansi looked back at Snake, and he never blinked. Anansi the Spider was a great liar.

"All right," agreed Snake, "measure me against the bamboo pole."

So Snake lay straight along the pathway, and Anansi put the long bamboo pole beside him. Anansi walked up and down, pushing and nudging so the Snake and the pole lay exactly side by side, touching. Then he walked up to Snake's head again.

"This won't work," said Anansi, "because if your tail is at one end, and I mark it, by the time I walk up to your head you can move up, so you will seem even longer, and I can't get a true measurement."

"Then tie my tail," said Snake, "tie my tail to that end."

So Anansi took a strong rope and tied Snake's tail to one end of the bamboo. Then he walked back to Snake's head.

"Your tail hold fast?" said Anansi.

"Yes".

"Now stretch out," said Anansi, "stretch out, hard as you can, and we see how far your nose can reach."

Snake stretched and stretched and stretched, and Anansi waited until Snake's eyes were closed from stretching. Then quick as a flash, he tied Snake's head to the pole as well. Then he ran to the middle and put in another tie, and another, and scampered up and down tying Snake to the pole until he couldn't move an inch.

Snake was captured. The word spread through the forest like a fire, Monkey told it to Parrot, and Parrot told it to Bear, and Bear told it to Tiger, and pretty soon they had all gathered to see Snake, tied to the bamboo pole. Anansi was there, boasting away. "I am great," boasted Anansi, "I am greater than grater cake, from now on I am the Storyteller, and all the animal stories are Anansi Stories."

Anansi and the Old Higue

Anansi finds a new way of tricking his friends. He frightens them with stories of an evil witch called the Old Higue.

Anansi tells them they must not bad mouth *each other. Can you guess what that means? Look in the glossary to see if you are right.*

Anansi had a problem. He couldn't understand why he was so poor. Everybody else in the village had pigs and goats and chicken, fruit, vegetables and such. Anansi had nothing. He was so worried about the problem that he couldn't leave his bed. Why was he so poor? Day after day he stayed at home, straining his brain, trying to master the matter. He was the smartest person in the village, so why was he so poor?

Thinking made him hungry. The fruit that he could liberate from other people's trees, or the vegetables he could dig from other people's grounds was not enough to satisfy him. His stomach was always quarrelling, begging for more. He wanted roast chicken, suckling pig, and curry goat. He thought about food until his mouth watered, but he didn't get off his bed.

Then one day he had an idea, a plan for getting rich. It meant doing a little work, but not too much. First of all, Anansi went down to the market. He sat near the entrance, holding his head in his hands and looking sorrowful. Every once in a while, he would sigh and say, "Terrible thing, Oh what a terrible thing!" Then he would shake his head sadly.

Brer Tiger, who was a kind-hearted soul, noticed Anansi creating and carrying on, muttering to himself. At first, Tiger thought Anansi was mad, then he thought it must be a toothache. Anyway, he went over to Anansi and asked politely what the matter was.

"Terrible times. Terrible times are coming, Brer Tiger!" said Anansi in a voice of doom.

"Is that so?" said Tiger.

"I had a dream," continued Anansi, in his parson's voice. "I dreamed of the Old Higue."

Tiger was suspicious of Anansi, but he was as frightened of Old Higue as anybody else. He knew Old Higue could leave her skin behind and travel as a ball of fire, and that she sucked the blood of the innocent.

"What did you dream, Anansi?" Tiger asked, and sat down beside him.

Anansi looked sideways at Tiger. Then he put on his holy voice again. "Old Higue appeared to me in a dream. She said that if the people around here continued to bad mouth one another, to say evil things about their neighbours, to laugh and mock at their friends, she, the Old Higue, would come to haunt this place."

Tiger knew what happened when a village was haunted by the Old Higue. Sometimes it got so bad the people ran away, leaving their houses empty, and their fields to be overgrown by bush.

"You swear you had this dream, Anansi?" he asked.

"Would I tell you a lie?" said Anansi.

The word spread through the market like fire in a cane field. The bad mouthing had to stop, or the Old Higue was coming. You never saw such a lot of happy, smiling folk, wishing each other well, congratulating one another, smiling and laughing. Dog spoke to Rat. Rat bowed to Cat. Horse told Donkey what a wonderful singing voice he had. Brer Goat told Brer Pig that he was slim and handsome. Anansi was satisfied. The first part of the plan was working.

Anansi went home. He found his machete under his bed. He put a new handle on his rusted hoe. Then he sat outside, sharpening his tools and whistling cheerfully. His neighbours passed by, waving and smiling.

"Hello Tiger, Howdydo Dog, good to see you Goat!" and so on.

They all nodded and smiled, and remarked to each other how nice it was to see Anansi, what an industrious fellow he was, and what a shame he was so poor. So far so good.

Next day, Anansi took himself and his tools to a place by the roadside named "Barren Ground". It was as barren as the name, scorched by the sun, the soil all washed away, nothing but rockstone and macca bush. Anansi set to work, digging.

Dog was the first to pass by. He could see Anansi working, sweat pouring off him. Anansi didn't seem to mind that his hoe was clanging and bouncing off the rocks. He was just working away and singing a digging song:

> "Hold him Joe
> Hold him Joe
> Me donkey want water
> Hold him Joe . . ."

"Anansi," said Dog, "what you doing?"

Anansi wiped the sweat from his forehead. "I'm preparing the land," said Anansi, "I'm going to plant corn and peas."

Dog nearly died laughing. "Anansi, you must be the world's biggest idiot. Only a fool would plant peas in rockstone."

Anansi looked sadly at Dog. "Dog, my friend, you are bad mouthing me."

At which, Dog began to tremble, because he remembered about the Old Higue coming to haunt the village.

"I'm sorry, Anansi."

"Sorry can't set a broken bone," said Anansi. "Perhaps a little gift to the Old Higue would be in order. I know where she is, and I could take it to her."

"I'll give her some corn and peas," suggested Dog.

Anansi looked doubtful. "You know what the Old Higue is like. She wants meat. Don't you have a new litter of pigs?"

"Good idea!" said Dog. "I'll give her a suckling pig."

So that night Dog came round to Anansi's house with a present of corn and peas and a suckling pig, which Anansi put in his yard. Anansi warned him not to tell anybody about it in case he got into trouble for his bad mouthing.

Next day, Anansi was back in Barren Ground, waiting for somebody to pass by. When he saw Tiger coming, he started chopping furiously with his machete. Tiger stopped to watch him. The sweat was pouring from Anansi's brow, and the sparks were flying from the stones. Anansi was singing:

"... Just as the chicken dem
Follow de hen
So de woman dem
Follow de men ..."

"What are you doing, Anansi?" said Tiger.

"I'm preparing the land," replied Anansi, "I'm going to plant corn and peas."

"Anansi, you couldn't be so stupid, so you must be a liar."

No sooner had he said it, than Tiger remembered about the Old Higue, and clapped his hand to his mouth. Anansi shook his head sadly.

"I see you remember. What are we going to do?"

Tiger didn't want to be the one who brought trouble on the whole village, so he considered the matter.

"Suppose I give the Old Higue a present?" said Tiger.

"Correct." said Anansi.

"I could give her some yams, and cho-choes."

"You know what that old woman is like, Brer Tiger, she likes meat."

So that night, Tiger came round to Anansi's house with a present of yams and cho-choes, and a goat ready for the pot, which Anansi put in his yard. Anansi warned him not to tell anybody about it in case he got into trouble for his bad mouthing.

The next one to fall in the trap was Brer Goat, whose present was a basket of chickens. Soon, Anansi's kitchen was like a store room, full of fruit and vegetables, and his yard was like a zoo. Everything was cackling and honking, and braying and neighing, and squealing and grunting at everything else. Anansi's neighbours wondered how it could have happened. Anansi, who was so poor, was now the richest person in the village.

It was Brer Tiger, who had been suspicious all along, who put two and two together, and figured out that they had all been tricked. The next question was what to do about Anansi. Dog wanted to burn his house down, and give him beating. Goat wanted to throw him out of the village. Tiger said that might make the Old Higue vexed, and cause them even more trouble. Brer Turkey said the Old Higue didn't come into it. Even so, they shouldn't dirty their hands by attacking Anansi. He had an idea. He told them about it, and they all agreed to give Turkey's idea a chance.

Next day, Anansi was back in Barren Ground, resting in the shade of a rock. When he heard Turkey coming he jumped up, grabbed his hoe, and started banging on the rocks, singing his digging song:

"Hold him Joe
Hold him Joe
Me donkey wan' water
Hold him Joe . . ."

Turkey paid no mind; he just kept strolling along on the other side of the road. Anansi banged harder and sang louder, but Turkey paid no attention, walking along and whistling. Finally, Anansi could stand it no longer.

"Oi! Turkey!" he said.

"Oh. Brer Anansi," said Turkey, "I'm sorry I didn't see you."

"How do you mean, you didn't see me? Are you deaf? Are you blind?"

"Oh no, Anansi, nothing like that. I was in a hurry. I have to get to town to get my hair cut. The barber is waiting for me."

Anansi looked at Turkey's bald head and laughed. He dropped the hoe and the machete and rocked with laughter. He held his belly, and roared.

'Turkey, you're a damn fool, man! How are you going to get a haircut? You're as bald as an egg!"

Turkey turned red. "So, Brer Anansi, I've caught you. Why are you mocking me? Bad mouthing me? What shall we say to the Old Higue? What present shall we give her? You go home, and give all the things you have taken from Goat, Tiger, and Dog, and the others. Give them all back. If not, they will be coming for you tonight, and that will be worse than any Old Higue!"

Anansi did that.

And from that day to this, nobody laughs at Brer Turkey's bald head.

Anansi and the Alligator Eggs

One time, Brer Anansi got a job working for Brer Man. He was supposed to bend down and weed out Brer Man's yam patch. As soon as the sun got hot, Anansi began to feel tired. So he left the weeds to carry on growing, lay down under a breadfruit tree and fell fast asleep. Brer Man came looking for him, to see how the work was getting on. Anansi was fast asleep under the breadfruit tree. Brer Man started shouting and complaining so Anansi opened one eye and looked at him.

"Why you not working, Anansi?"

"Hungry," said Anansi, "Empty bag can't stand up."

Brer Man was a kind-hearted soul, so he sent out for some dinner for Anansi, saltfish, ackee and boiled bananas. Anansi stuffed himself with the dinner, lay down under the breadfruit tree and went back to sleep. Later on, Brer Man came looking for him again, to see how the work was going, and found Anansi fast asleep.

"Why you not working, Anansi? I sent you a good dinner."

"That's true," said Anansi, "that's why. Full bag can't bend."

So Brer Man washed his hands of Anansi and left him right there under the breadfruit tree. Pretty soon, Anansi woke up because the pangs of hunger began to bite him again. But he was too lazy to move. He just lay on his back listening to the birds. Then he realized the birds were talking about food, so he listened more carefully. Brer Pigeon was telling Brer Ground Dove and Brer Blue Quit about a dokanoo tree he had found full of huge ripe, juicy dokanoos. Anansi's mouth began to water. He loved dokanoos more than salvation. Brer Grass Quit, Brer Parraqueet, and Brer Pechary all joined in to talk about this wondrous dokanoo tree. Where could it be? Anansi couldn't bear it any longer.

"Oh, birds," he said, sweet as sugar, "I am Anansi, your cousin Anansi, here at the bottom of the tree. Tell me, for I am your cousin, and love you all, where is the dokanoo tree?"

"On an island in the river," said Grass Quit.

"You can't go there, Anansi," said Pechary, "the river is full of alligators.

Anansi would do anything to get to the dokanoos, but he was mightily afraid of alligators, just the thought of them, drifting around disguised as logs, snapping up crabs in those huge jaws made Anansi shiver.

"You would have to fly, Anansi," said Grass Quit, "and you can't do that."

"You have no feathers," said the Ground Dove.

"Well, my cousins, my friends," said Brer Anansi, "you can help me. Each of you give me a feather, you won't miss it, and I'll make a set of wings."

The birds chattered among themselves, amused by Anansi's idea. They agreed. Each of them plucked a feather and let it fall to Anansi. Anansi gathered up the feathers, got some gum from the logwood tree, and made a set of wings. The birds watched. Then Anansi put on the wings, climbed a post, jumped off, and fell on his head. The birds laughed. But they were kind-hearted creatures, and they offered to teach Anansi how to fly. They gave him instructions, and flapped about to show him how. Anansi was determined to get to the dokanoos, and he tried and tried, and tried again.

At last, he could fly, not so well, but well enough. So with the birds for company, Anansi set off to fly to the island in the river. They flew along with him, chirping away, giving advice, and Anansi flapped his wings for dear life. Halfway across the river, Anansi looked down from a great height, and saw the water swarming with alligators. He was so frightened his wings missed a beat and he went into a steep dive, straightening out just in time to reach the island, and land in the dokanoo tree.

Anansi had never seen such dokanoos, big, luscious, juicy, and perfectly ripe. He set about gobbling them down, eating and filling his crocus bag at the same time. He was so greedy he started pushing the birds out of the way.

"That's mine," said Anansi, "I saw that one first, get out of my way," and so on.

The birds began to get angry. After all, they had taken pity on him and taught him how to fly, and now he was trying to hog all the dokanoos. They quarrelled with him, but Anansi kept on with his greedy behaviour. The birds got vexed, and each one plucked out the feather he had given out of Anansi's wings, and flew away with it. Anansi was left alone in the dokanoo tree. He didn't mind. He was eating and filling his bag at the same time, and he didn't care. After a while, he climbed down out of the tree, and only then did he realize that he was in trouble. How was he going to get back across the river? Anansi didn't like alligators. He was terrified of alligators, of their evil double-lidded eyes and interlocking teeth.

Never mind, he went bravely to the river bank. Brer Alligator was cruising by.

"Hello!" called out Brer Anansi, "Hello, Brer Alligator, this is your cousin Anansi."

Alligator came slowly toward him. Anansi's knees were knocking, but he kept smiling. "Cousin Alligator," he said, "remember me, Anansi, your friend?"

Alligator just looked at him.

"I'm in a little bit of trouble here," continued Anansi, "I have to get across the river, but I lost my boat. You couldn't as a gracious favour, just let me stand on your back, and you swim across?"

Alligator waddled ashore, and Anansi climbed aboard, still clutching his bag of dokanoos. Alligator set off into midstream with Anansi standing on his rough, horny back, praying for dry land.

Halfway across, Brer Alligator spoke. "I don't see you much, Anansi, I hardly see you at all."

"I'm very busy these days," said Anansi, "what with one thing and another."

"Still, you're here now, you must come see my house."

Anansi did not dare to say no, so Alligator carried him to his house under a high bank of the river. They had to dive down and up again, but inside the house it was bright, roomy and comfortable, though Anansi didn't like the smell of Alligator. Then Anansi saw Alligator looking at him in a hungry fashion, and his knees started knocking again.

"Brer Alligator," he said, "I hope you are hungry, because I brought this bag of dokanoos especially for you."

Alligator was pleased, and gobbled up the precious dokanoos with Anansi watching, sadly, his mouth watering.

"Now," said Alligator, "I'll show you the rest of the house, and he showed Anansi the back room where he kept his eggs. There were twelve of them, and Anansi's eyes lit up when he saw them.

"Come," said Alligator, "you must help me to wash the eggs. They have to be washed every day and then put back in the warm." Together they carried the eggs to the water's edge in a basket.

"You wash," said Anansi, "I'll pass them to you one by one and count them as they come back. One."

"One," said Alligator, washing the egg.

Anansi, just behind him put one in his mouth same time, and swallowed it straight down.

"Two," said Anansi, passing an egg.

"Two," said Alligator, washing it. Same time Anansi was gulping another one down and putting a stone in the basket.

"Three," said Anansi.

"Three," said Alligator, washing while Anansi ate.

And so right up to twelve, because while Anansi was eating the eggs, he was passing the same one back every time, just rubbing it in the mud, and giving it back to Alligator. And each time he put a stone in the basket. So of the twelve eggs there was only one remaining. Alligator took the basket and put it back in the back room.

"Thank you, Anansi," said Alligator, "Now I will send you on to shore. So saying, he called out for Brer Tarpon and Brer Snook who lived in the river, and they came with a boat.

"Just do me a favour," said Alligator, "provide a conveyance for my cousin Anansi, and take him to shore."

No sooner said than done, and Tarpon and Snook were rowing Anansi to shore. Anansi was so pleased with himself. He was on his way to safety, and his belly was full of Alligator's eggs . . . then there came the most almighty howling from Alligator's house. He had discovered what Anansi had done, tricked him, and left him with one so-so egg. Anansi was almost ashore when he looked back to see Alligator coming lickety-split, churning up the water with his tail and calling out, "Anansi! Anansi, I'm coming for you!"

"What him say?" asked Brer Tarpon.

"He's just saying goodbye," said Anansi, "Row faster."

Just in time, Anansi jumped ashore, and ran for the forest. He didn't look back, and from that day to this Anansi doesn't go near Alligator.

Anansi and his Family

As happens to everybody, Anansi got married. His wife was named Crooksy, and she was a real pretty little something. They got along like a knife and fork. Crooksy did everything for Anansi, cleaned the house and swept the yard and cooked the food, and everything went along merrily.

But, as also happens, hard times came. Anansi and Crooksy were short, mostly of food, which was a thing Anansi couldn't bear. Now Crooksy had a pig that she kept in the yard, and the hungrier Anansi got the more his mind turned towards the pig. He dared not ask Crooksy to kill the pig, which was her prize possession, but the thought of roast pork was with him night and day, and the sight of the pig made him tremble.

Anansi got so anxious that he finally took to his bed. He lay there with his eyes closed, holding his belly and groaning. Crooksy did her best to look after him. She boiled up tea made from the leaf-of-life. She put cold flannels on his head, and hot poultices on his feet. Nothing worked. Anansi just lay there and groaned. Crooksy was at her wit's end.

"Crooksy," whispered Anansi, "I'm sinking fast. You must get the doctor."

So Crooksy set out to look for the doctor. As soon as she was gone, Anansi jumped out of the window and sprinted into the bush. So it was that Crooksy, coming along the road, met Anansi, disguised as a doctor, coming the other way. He was wearing a tall black hat, a long black coat, and carrying a black bag. Crooksy begged Anansi the doctor to come and see Anansi her husband.

Anansi agreed, "But on one condition," he said. "I must see the patient alone. Whatever it is, it may be catching."

At Anansi's house, behind closed doors, Anansi the doctor consulted with Anansi's empty bed. Then he came out to see Crooksy and deliver his verdict.

"Your husband is very sick," said Anansi, "and only one thing can save him. He has greeditis, a severe case, and the only cure for it is pork."

"Where am I to get pork?" said Crooksy, "Times are hard."

"As I was coming into the yard," said Anansi the doctor, "I saw a pig. You must kill the pig to save your husband."

So Crooksy did that, and Anansi got his bellyful of pork. But even Anansi couldn't eat it all. The pig was salted and spiced with pimento and pepper, and put to smoke over the fire. So it was that Anansi invented jerkpork.

As happens to everybody, Anansi and Crooksy had three children, and they were called Peckish, Hungry, and Starving-to-Death. Finding food for five people was a constant trial to Anansi. He liked his night's sleep, his morning rest, his midday rest, and his evening rest. But resting won't even boil water, so Anansi had to stir himself.

One morning, he set out early, in search of food for his family. Up and down the highways and byways he went. Breadfruit was out of season. The pear trees had been stripped. The ackees weren't ripe. He made a slingshot and fired it at the birds, but missed. He was too slow to catch a rabbit. He couldn't even find a stalk of sugar cane. All this made Anansi tired. So he laid down to rest in a shady spot, and slept through the heat of the day.

In the cool of the evening he started home again, walking slowly, wondering what he was going to tell Crooksy. Then, up ahead of him, Anansi saw Brer Rat, carrying a bunch of plantains on his head. It was a big bunch, so heavy that Rat was really struggling. Anansi quickened his step to catch up, and greeted him cheerfully.

"Hello, Brer Rat, how you coming?"

"Struggling," said Rat, "struggling along."

"What's that I see?" said Anansi, "Plantains?"

"Plantains," replied Rat. "I'm taking them home to my family."

"That's a fine, big bunch," said Anansi, admiringly.

"The last from my field," said Rat.

"You won't be able to eat all that."

"All that and more," said Rat, "it will have to last a long time."

"Poor me," said Anansi, "I'm going home empty-handed. I have nothing for my wife and children. Nothing at all."

"Hard cheese," Rat said, showing no sympathy.

"You know I never beg," begged Anansi, "but times are hard. If you could spare just one or two for the wife and children . . ."

Rat put the bunch of plantains down on the bank, and carefully broke off four of the smaller ones, and gave them to Anansi. Then he put the rest of the bunch back on his head and set off down the road.

"Wait, Brer Rat, wait! I have a wife and *three* children. That's five in all. You only give me four."

Rat paid no attention.

So Anansi went home with the four plantains. Crooksy made a fire, and roasted them, and they all sat down to eat. Anansi gave one to his wife, and one to each of the children. Then he sat and looked mournfully at his empty plate.

"What's happening?" said Peckish, "Daddy is not eating."

"It's all right," said Anansi, heroically, "the plantains are for you."

Peckish couldn't bear to see his father go without, so he gave half his plantain to Anansi. Hungry and Starving to Death copied their brother. Crooksy, seeing the generosity of the children, gave Anansi half of hers as well.

So Anansi had a bellyful, as usual.

Next day, they were all hungry again, and poor Anansi was pushed out of bed. He travelled the highways and byways looking for food. Then he heard that Brer Tiger was running a competition, giving away big prizes. It seems Tiger had a pasture which was overgrown in bush and he wanted it cleared. There was only one snag. The field was full of cow-itch, which is the worst kind of stinging nettle. Tiger was only giving prizes to anybody who could work all day without scratching. Brer Rat and Brer Dog had already taken up the challenge and were hard at work, with Tiger following them wherever they went to make sure they didn't scratch. That cow-itch was savage, and soon Rat and Dog were jumping around scratching themselves like they had St Vitus' Dance. Tiger sent them away empty-handed.

Anansi took up the challenge. He set to work in Tiger's field, clearing the bush. Tiger followed him everywhere he went to make sure he didn't scratch. Pretty soon, the cow-itch got Anansi in the shoulder, and his skin was burning. So he turned to Tiger and said,

"Tiger, is that a fly on your shoulder?"

"Where?" said Tiger.

"Just here," said Anansi, touching his itching shoulder.

While Tiger looked for the fly, Anansi scratched.

Pretty soon, the cow-itch got Anansi in the leg.

"Tiger," said Anansi, "is that a wasp on your knee?"

"Where?" said Tiger.

"Just here," said Anansi, touching his itching knee.

While Tiger looked for the wasp, Anansi scratched.

So Anansi worked all day, and Tiger never saw him scratch. Only Brer Anansi, and Brer Mongoose, who was so hairy the cow-itch never got to him, had been able to do it. Tiger had to give them their reward.

Tiger took Anansi and Mongoose to his house. He took them into a room and showed them two ropes hanging through the back window. One was a big, thick rope, and the other a thin, little one.

"There's a cow on the end of one rope, and a chicken on the other. Each of you choose a rope, and take what you get."

"You choose," said Mongoose, who didn't want any quarrel.

Anansi did some heavy thinking. "By rights, the chicken should be on the little rope, and the cow on the big rope," he thought. "But Tiger is a trickster, so he has changed the ropes." Confidently, Anansi took hold of the little rope, leaving the big rope for Brer Mongoose. Anansi was too clever. The big rope had the cow, and the little rope had the chicken. Anansi was so vexed he boxed the chicken's ears.

So they set off home, Brer Mongoose leading the cow, and Brer Anansi leading the chicken. It was a long way, and they were tired after all the work they had done for Tiger, so they sat down to rest. Brer Mongoose fell asleep. Quick as flash Anansi cut off the cow's tail. He buried one end of it in the ground, leaving the hairy part standing up, and waving in the breeze. Then he led the cow into the bushes and tied it up. When Mongoose woke up, all he saw of his cow was the tail sticking out of the ground. Anansi meanwhile was pretending to be asleep also. Mongoose woke him in distress.

"Anansi," said Mongoose, "look, look what has happened!"

"The cow is digging his way down," said Anansi, "Grab the tail and pull him out before he gets away."

So Mongoose pulled the cow's tail, and it came out of the ground.

"Bad luck," said Anansi, "you pulled off the tail, and the rest got away."

Mongoose was heartbroken. He had worked hard all day. He had got his reward. Now there was nothing left but a cow tail.

"Never mind," said Anansi, generously. "You take the chicken."

Mongoose couldn't believe his ears.

"Go on, take it," said Anansi. "I'll take the cow tail. It makes very good soup. You take the chicken."

So Mongoose took the chicken, and went home. From that day to this, Mongoose loves chicken, and he will do anything for chicken, even steal. Anansi went into the bush, found the cow, and took it home to Crooksy.

"There," said Anansi, "we can have a feast. A whole cow. Kill him and roast him."

"It's too big," said Crooksy.

"We can smoke it," said Anansi, "like the pig."

"Oh, you remember the pig," said Crooksy, "You remember how you play tricks on me, and eat my pig. Well, I'm not cooking this cow, I'm keeping it, as fair exchange for my pig. She is going to live in the yard, and give milk for the children."

"What about me?" said Anansi. "You expect me to drink milk?"

"You can look after yourself," said Crooksy, "that's your speciality."

From that day to this, Anansi doesn't try any more tricks on Crooksy.

Mrs Anansi Fights back

Crooksy decides to leave Anansi and look after herself. She is much more successful than Anansi has ever been – but who do you think wins in the end?

One day, Anansi was having a little rest in his favourite place under the mango tree. Crooksy, that's Anansi's wife, came marching out of the house. She was in a tearing temper.

"I'm sick and tired," she said, "I'm sick and tired of it."

Anansi opened one eye. Crooksy had been as jumpy as a flea recently, so Anansi knew he had to tread softly.

"Of what, darling?" he said.

"I'm sick unto death!" said Crooksy.

"Of what?"

"Exploitation."

Anansi sat up. He put his back against the tree in case Crooksy attacked him from behind. "Exploitation" was a word that Anansi had heard at the rum shop and at political meetings. It was not something he expected to hear from a woman, least of all from his own dearly beloved Crooksy.

"I'm sick of it!" she said, taking off her apron and throwing it in the dirt.

"I still don't know what you're talking about," Anansi said.

"Exploitation means that I work while you sleep under the mango tree. That's what I'm talking about. I get up in the morning, and bathe and wash the children. I cook the meals. I wash the clothes. I clean the house and sweep the yard. I dig the garden and reap the crops. I go to market. And when I have spare time, I go and work for Brer Tiger's wife to get the odd halfpenny. I do all of this while you sleep under the mango tree."

"But I'm out of a job," Anansi replied reasonably. "Times are hard, I can't get work."

"Times are always hard for me. I do all the work, and I'm not even somebody. I'm Mrs Anansi. I don't even have a name of my own."

Anansi's mind was boggling. "Mrs Anansi is a name. Mrs Anansi is a nice name," he said, weakly.

"I want to be myself!" Crooksy shouted.

There was no answer to that.

"I want to find myself."

"But you're not lost," protested Anansi. "Crooksy, darling, you're standing right in front of me."

"I want to be equal. I'll get a job and look after myself. You can stay home and look after the children. See how you like it."

Anansi considered the matter carefully. He looked at Crooksy, standing there with her arms akimbo. She wasn't foaming at the mouth, but she had a funny look in her eye. He remembered that when Brer Mongoose went mad they made a strait-jacket out of an old pillow case. He didn't have one. He didn't even have an old plastic fertilizer sack.

"Crooksy," Anansi said, "you've been talking to somebody. You've been talking to one of those fat white women with curlers in their hair."

"No," said Crooksy. "I've been thinking."

That was the last straw. Anansi lay down again in the hammock and closed his eyes. Crooksy was cuckoo. The world had come to an end. But if he were going to die, at least he would die in his sleep.

Next day, Crooksy packed her belongings in a suitcase, and took the bus to the city. Anansi and his three children, Peckish, Hungry, and Starving-to-Death, were left alone, helpless and defenceless against the world. What were they to do, and how were they to eat?

First of all, Anansi collected sticks and lit a fire. He boiled some water. He couldn't find any cocoa, so he and the children had hot water for breakfast, with sugar in it. Then they had a consultation. There was no food in the house, and no money. Peckish said that was the same as always. Hungry said Crooksy had always been able to find something for them to eat. Starving-to-Death just cried. Anansi tried to explain to them that women made meals out of nothing by magic. Men couldn't do it. The children suggested that he get a job. Anansi explained that times were hard, the sun was hot, and with nothing in his belly he hadn't even the strength to look for work.

He explained to the children that as Crooksy had weighed anchor and left them, they had to look after themselves. He gave them each a white stick, and a tin cup, and sent them into town. Peckish, Hungry and Starving-to-Death thought it was a big joke, and they went tap-tapping around all day holding out their cups for pennies. Peckish, who was big and strong, didn't do so well. Hungry, who was middling, did better. Starving-to-Death, who was a pitiful looking little thing, collected lots of money. That night, they brought home bully beef, bread, and condensed milk, and they all had a feast.

But the news soon went out that Anansi was sending his children out to beg. They were pretending to be blind, but they could see as well as anybody. The pennies stopped dropping into the little tin cups. Anansi had to think of another idea. He put a sign around their necks saying "Mother gone", but it didn't work. Everybody patted the children on the shoulder and said "Sorry". But sorry can't buy bully beef.

Peckish worked out a plan that even Anansi was proud of. The three children went into town, and into a busy street, where the cars were moving very slowly. Peckish slapped the wing of a car and shouted "Oi!". At the same time Hungry lay down in the gutter. Then Starving-to-Death ran up to the driver shouting, "You killed my brother! You killed my brother!" Then Peckish said, "Don't worry, it's only a broken leg. Give him five dollars." The trick worked well on men drivers, especially tourists, but it didn't fool the women. The women would just say, "Stop telling lies, and go home to your mother."

The children tried everything, from going around with a bandaged dog to collecting for motherless children. It was all they could do to keep body and soul together. Meanwhile, Anansi, who was feeling the pinch, went to consult with Brer Rat. Rat had no sympathy for him at all.

"Anansi, you're not a man, you're a mouse," said Rat. "You get on the bus, go to the city, find Crooksy, and give her a good beating."

"It won't work," said Anansi, "I'm weak from lack of food. I couldn't beat a carpet."

"Then get another woman," said Rat.

"They're not easy to find," said Anansi, "not nowadays."

"What about Sister Pea Dove?" asked Rat. "She's lonesome."

"No," said Anansi, "I know her well."

"She's pretty," said Rat.

"True. But she wants clothes and shoes, and things like that. Cooking gives her a headache, and she can't clean because she has a bad back. All she wants is dancing and jollification."

"What are you going to do?" said Rat.

Anansi went home to think about it, and fell asleep under the mango tree.

When he woke up, Crooksy was standing in front of him. She had a smart suit, jacket and skirt, and a silk scarf tied around her neck. She had big ear rings and horn-rimmed glasses. She was carrying a little black briefcase with a combination lock on it.

"Welcome home," said Anansi.

"I've come back . . ." Crooksy began.

"I'm hungry," Anansi said.

". . . for the children," continued Crooksy. She pointed to an enormous motor car outside the gate, with a chauffeur standing beside it. "I'm taking them to live with me in the city."

Anansi looked at the motor car. "Is that yours?"

"Yes, it is," said Crooksy.

"Then you are rich?"

"You could say."

"Then you did the right thing. Water under the bridge, Crooksy. I will forgive you. I'll come and live with you and the children. You can go out to work and I will stay at home – just like you wanted."

At which they hugged and squeezed and so on. Then Anansi put his belongings in the back of the car, and went to look for the children.

Crooksy had done well. She had started by selling yams in the market place. Then she opened a shop, and then a supermarket. Soon after she went into buying and selling houses, importing curry powder from India and things like that. Crooksy had money. She had a big house overlooking the city, with a terrace and a swimming pool. There was a cook, a maid, and a gardener. The big car had a garage, and the chauffeur came every morning at half past seven. Crooksy had black coffee and yoghurt for breakfast and left for the office at a quarter to eight. The car came back at half past to take the children to school. Peckish, Hungry, and Starving-to-Death learned to read and write. They were sleek and fat, and their uniforms were washed and pressed every morning. Anansi would wave good bye from the bedroom window before lying down again for his morning nap.

Anansi was in his element. About ten he would get up and put on his white shorts and his Adidas shirt and settle down to breakfast, oranges, bacon, eggs, breadfruit, plantain, saltfish and ackee, toast and guava jelly. Then he would go down to the barber's for a shave and a manicure. About twelve he would meet with Brer Pig and Brer Parakeet down at the hotel for lobsters and planter's punch. Then the chauffeur would take him home for his afternoon nap. In the evening, Crooksy usually had some business or other to do. So Anansi played ping-pong with the children, swam in the pool, and entertained his old friends from the country.

Brer Mongoose had been let out of the mad house, and he was a frequent visitor. Brer Rat, whose children had grown up and scattered, came for days at a time. Brer Jackass was always there, expressing his silly opinions, and Brer Tiger, who was getting fat, sleepy and slow, dropped anchor in Anansi's deepest chair.

"This is the life, Anansi!" said Tiger.

"True," said Anansi, putting his feet up.

"You've found the secret," said Rat.

"True," said Anansi, gazing at the sunset.

"I know what it is," said Jackass loudly, "Women should not be exploited. We should set them free – let them go to work."

"She does have me always to lean upon," Anansi said.

"That's true," said Rat, "she couldn't do it without you."

"Children getting on well at school? They're such pretty little things," said Parakeet.

"Oh yes," Anansi said, "they're smart. They take after their mother."

"I worry about Crooksy," Tiger said, shifting his great weight, "she works too hard. One day she'll drop dead."

"Oh no," Anansi said, "She loves it. She's a free woman. All you fellows should do it. You should let your wives go out to work."